I0771484

To Amanda,
Kim, and Leslie

First published in 2024
Written by Melissa Avstreih
Book design by Bryony van der Merwe

ISBN: 979-8-9911846-0-1 (hardcover)
ISBN: 979-8-9911846-1-8 (paperback)
ISBN: 979-8-9911846-2-5 (e-book)

GOODNIGHT Menopause

Melissa Avstreih

In a 60-degree room
There was
an air conditioner
And a fan

And a wide-awake woman...
z-z-z
Glaring at a sleeping man

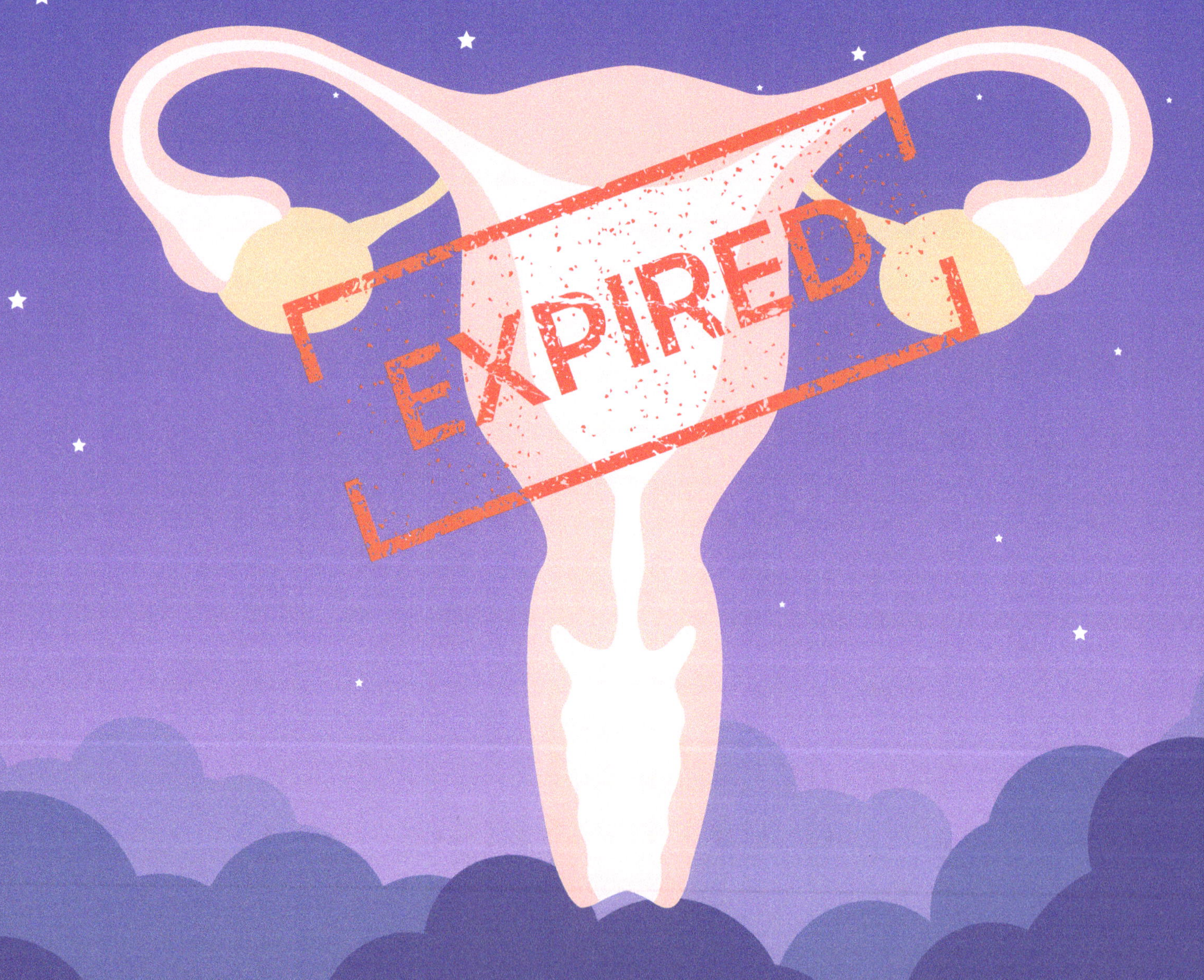

And there were
shriveled-up eggs

and a pair
of hot legs

And a nightgown that clings

And pills for mood swings

And a growing
waistline

And estrogen in decline

And a phone and
a brush and cheeks
that were flush

And a middle-aged lady
who was whispering...
fuck

Goodnight room
Goodnight fan

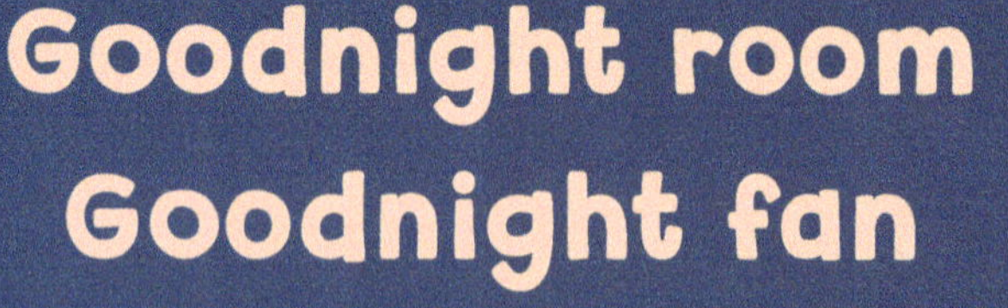

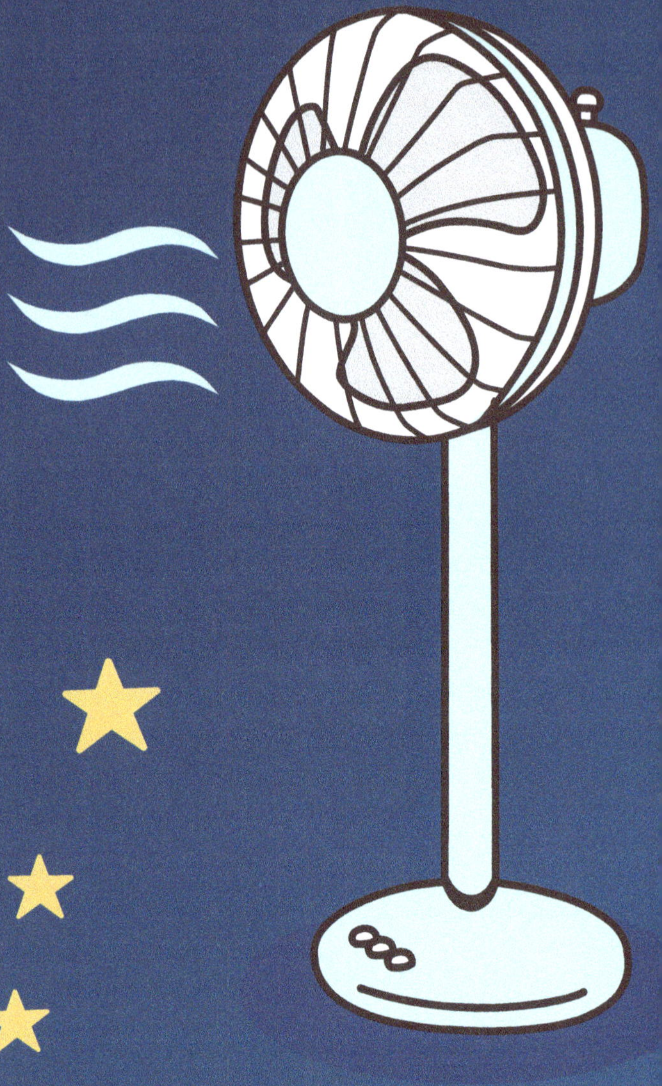

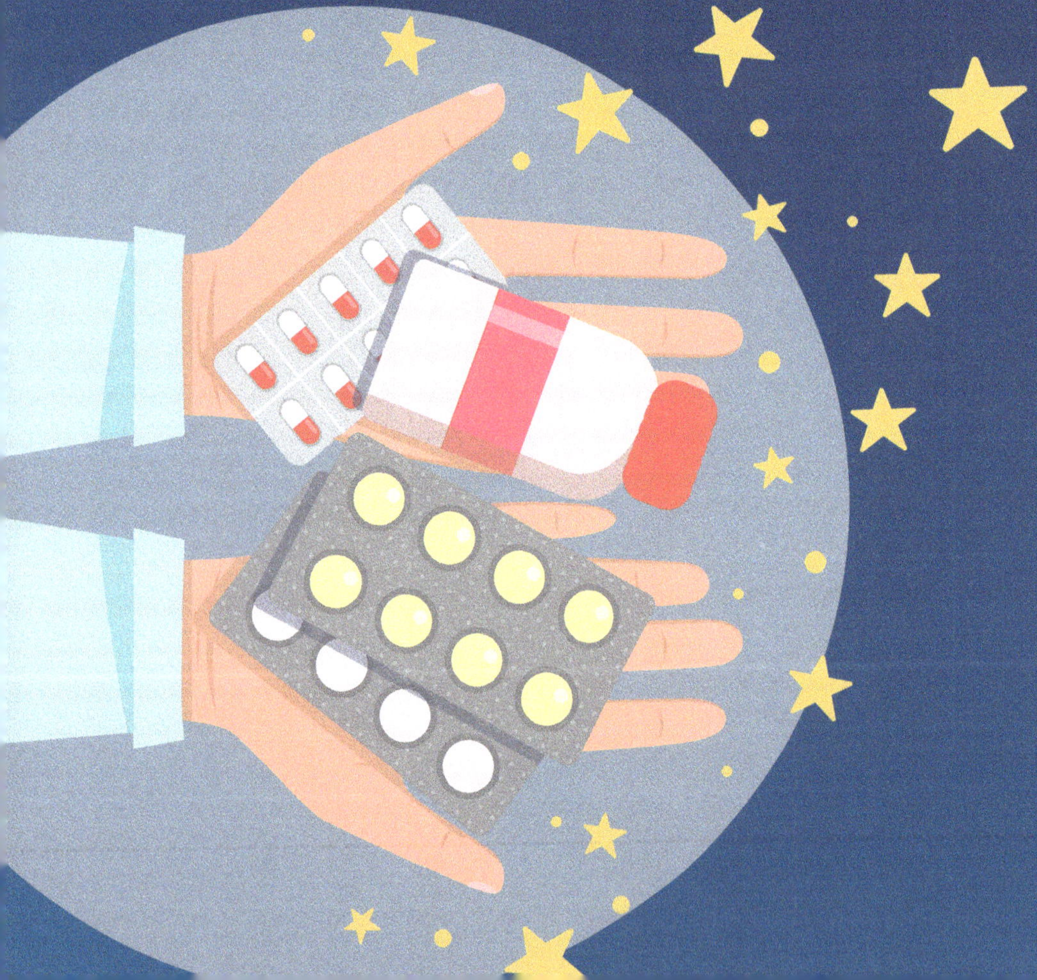

Goodnight
Wellbutrin
and Ativan

Goodnight A/C
and the sleeping man

Goodnight
gray hair

Goodnight mean glare

Goodnight foggy brain

And goodnight
weight gain

Goodnight irritability

And goodnight fertility

Goodnight incontinence

And goodnight
vaginal dryness

Goodnight phone
And goodnight brush

Goodnight
nightgown

Goodnight gut

And goodnight to the middle-aged
lady whispering "fuck"

Goodnight
stars

Goodnight air

Goodnight
women
everywhere

About the Author

Melissa Avstreih finds inspiration in the simplest life moments. One dark and sweaty night, she had the idea for Goodnight Menopause after an evening with a group of friends discussing the physical changes of - that's right--menopause. As the author of this little gem, Melissa's innate talents as wordsmith shine through.

A native of Norristown, Penn., Melissa has lived in the Washington, D.C., metro area since 1999. After a stint on Capitol Hill, she transitioned to journalism, working for a major national news service and earning a journalism degree from Harvard University. Now a senior communications pro at a federal agency, Melissa spends her free time indulging her passion for writing.

A relative newcomer to the publishing omniverse, Melissa has three new books in the offing. Seashells of the Jersey Shore will be released in Spring 2025. (Schiffer Publishing). Her second and third books in this series (under contract) will be released in 2026-27. Melissa lives (and writes) in Arlington, Va., with her husband and two sons.